W9-AEW-136

Four Scary Stories

by Tony Johnston
pictures by Tomie de Paola

G. P. Putnam's Sons / New York

For my three little things,
Jenny, Samantha, and Roger
And for Mom, who can wiggle her ears.

Text copyright © 1978 by Tony Johnston
Illustrations copyright © 1978 by Tomie de Paola
All rights reserved. Published simultaneously
in Canada by Longman Canada Limited, Toronto.
Printed in the United States of America

Library of Congress Cataloging in Publication Data
Johnston, Tony. Four scary stories.
SUMMARY: An imp, a goblin, a scalawag, and a boy
tell each other scary stories.
I. De Paola, Thomas Anthony.   II. Title.
PZ7.J6478Fo   [E]   77-13027
ISBN 0-399-20614-0

One night three little things met in a dark place—an imp, a goblin, and a scalawag. They wiped their little pointed feet, hung up their little pointed hats, and sat down to listen with their little pointed ears. And what did they listen to? Well, scary stories, of course. And what were the scariest stories they could think of? Well, BOY stories, of course.

"Me first," said the imp.

"Me first," said the goblin.

"No, me first," said the scalawag.

"If everyone is first, then no one is first," said the goblin. "So how about you second and you third and me first?"

"How about you two last and *me* first?" suggested the scalawag.

The imp stamped his little pointed feet and shouted, "ME FIRST!" so loudly that the others changed their minds. And he was first.

The Imp's Story

On a night black as ink, what do you think? A little imp heard a noise outside his window. So what did he do? He threw a flower pot at it. *Smash!*

Throwing a flower pot was so much fun that he grabbed a cuckoo clock and threw that too.

Bang! The clock broke to smithereens. The cuckoo cuckooed wildly. And that was fine.

So without stopping to listen for the noise, the imp looked around and saw all kinds of things to toss out.

Heave! Out went the pot-bellied stove. *Ho!* And the rocking chair. And the mat. And his hat.

Oh! It was very exciting. But when the dishes went, well, they made the best clatter of all.

"Hooray for the dishes!" cheered the imp.

Finally he had everything out and was feeling pretty good about it. So he sat down to rest. (Of course he sat down on nothing, because there was nothing left to sit on.)

And just then—he heard the noise again!
Oh, how he jumped! For now the noise was *inside!*

"Something's here," he thought. And all in a dither, he tried to hide.

First he tried to hide under the rug. But the rug was in the garden.

He tried to hide in the bathtub. But that was in the trees.

"Where?" he thought wildly. "Where can I hide?"

Under the bed. But, no! It was gone, gone, *gone*.

Just at that moment, a BOY appeared.
"*Yikes!*" cried the little imp.
Now he didn't want to hide at all. He wanted to get away.

So he tossed himself out the window too. And how he ran! He almost flew.
And he was so scared, he is probably running still.

That was such a scary story that the goblin, the scalawag, and even the imp himself shrieked and hid in a big kettle by the fire. They all laughed. And their voices were very big inside the kettle. Big and scary. And they loved that.

"My turn," said the goblin, hopping out.

"No, mine," said the scalawag, right behind.

"No, mine," said the imp loudly in his pointed ear.

"You just had a turn," scowled the scalawag.

"I know," said the imp. "I was trying to settle the argument."

"Who's arguing?" growled the scalawag.

"You," howled the goblin.

"Well, I'm not," said the imp.

"Oh, yes you are. You argue just for fun."

"Well, the most fun will be when I sock you one, you melon head!"

"Melon!" cried the goblin. "That reminds me of a scary story."

And he started before anyone else could.

The Goblin's Story

Have you ever heard of moon melons? Well, they soak up all the moonshine and glow like anything. And sweet? Mercy! And magic too. All you do is start them rolling, and they roll on and on.

Once a fat goblin was gathering moon melons when somebody said, "Who's taking my melons?"

The somebody was hiding behind a tree. So the goblin thought he was hearing things. And he went on gathering.

Then the somebody said, "These are my melons. They do what I want. Roll along, melons." And he pushed them.

Right then and there the melons began to roll away—slipping, sliding, glowing, gliding—through the silvery field!

"You can't do that!" cried the fat goblin.

So he chased them. And the moon melons rolled merrily along. They slipped around a tree. So did the goblin. They slithered under a fence. So did the goblin. They rumbled up and down the melon rows.

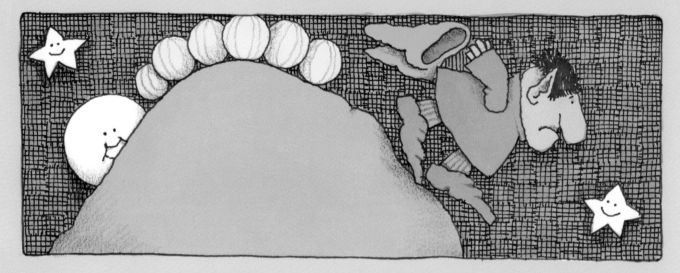

The goblin waddled behind them so fast that he might have caught them all. But the moon melons came to the top of a hill and stopped. The goblin was so fat, he went waddling right past them—down, down the hill. His hat whisked off. He could not stop!

Then a BOY sneaked out from behind the tree and gave those melons a push.

"After him!" he yelled.

Off thundered the moon melons, with the goblin puffing like the breeze and screeching, "Help! Help! Help!", which didn't help at all.

The fat goblin felt thinner and thinner. And very puffed. But the moon melons rolled on. And they were just about to knock him over when—he squeezed down a hole and was safe.

Up jumped the boy, laughing in the moonlight, "That will teach you to take my melons!"

Then the boy went home, rolling the moon melons along.

When the goblin saw that, he stamped his feet and shook his fist at the melons he had missed.

The scalawag, the imp, and even the goblin himself were so scared by that scary story that they shrieked and hid under the rug.

"Now it's my turn," mumbled the scalawag under the rug.

No one argued. The scalawag was worried when no one argued.

"It's my turn," he announced louder still.

The imp and the goblin waited for him to start. The scalawag waited for them to argue.

Finally, the imp stamped his little pointed feet and shouted, "HURRY UP AND TAKE YOUR TURN!" so loudly that the scalawag did.

The Scalawag's Story

A young scalawag was tramping along, doing nothing wrong, when he saw a magic hat. He knew it was magic because of the way it wiggled—all by itself.

So he put it on and sat down to see just what magic would happen.

He sat and sat. Nothing magic happened.

But suddenly—something very magic happened. A ghost came right out of the hat, curling like smoke, and tied itself in a knot—right around the scalawag's middle. And it would not let go. Not for anything.

The scalawag hooted and hollered. He danced and pranced. And he rolled all over the ground. But the ghost would not let go. It just laughed and laughed. And it tied itself in another knot besides. And squeezed. So the scalawag screamed like anything.

Then a BOY came from nowhere and shouted, "So there you
are! Untie yourself!" For it was his pet ghost.

Then he washed the ghost—rub, rub, rub—and hung it up like
a handkerchief. And it glowed and cried,
"WOOOOOOOooooo!" For it was very cold.

"Now I will wash *you*!" said the boy. And he tried to catch the
scalawag.

The boy got very close. The scalawag got very scared.

Just then he saw his own magic hat lying near. So he grabbed
it, quickly said, "Zinky, zinky, zoo," and—poof! He was gone.

The scalawag popped out under a toadstool far away. He
looked all around and saw—no one.
"I've never had a bath, and I never will!" he giggled.

The imp, the goblin, and even the scalawag himself were so scared at that close call that they shrieked and jumped into each other's laps.

Then they heard something in the dark. So they stopped shrieking and wiggled their little pointed ears to listen to what it was.

The goblin whispered, "Something new is here."
"What?" whispered the imp.
"I don't know."
"Well, poke it and find out."
"You poke it," whispered the goblin. "It's next to you."
So he poked it and jumped back fast.
"Ouch!" yelled the something new.
"It's an ouch," whispered the scalawag.
"It's a *boy*," whispered the something new.
The three little things shrieked, grabbed their little pointed hats, quickly said, "Zinky, zinky, zoo," and—poof! They were gone.

"Come back!" cried the boy.

"Never!" cried three voices near the ceiling.

"How did you get here?" asked the scalawag voice.

"I tiptoed," explained the boy.

"Sneaked," grumbled the imp voice.

"How long have you been listening?" asked the goblin voice.

"A long time," said the boy. "I'm a good listener."

"You're a sneaky listener," said the imp voice. "Why are you here?"

"To hear the stories. I didn't mean to scare you."

"Who's scared?" said the scalawag voice. "We just like to jump."

"Well, I just like you," said the boy. "Please come back. And I'll tell a scary story too."

"Mumble, mumble, buzz." They thought it over. And—poof! They were back, hanging in midair.

"I never tell stories to people in midair," said the boy. "It's not cozy."

"Who wants to be cozy with a boy?" asked the scalawag.

"I do for a scary story," said the imp, floating down.

"Me, too," said the goblin.

"Nuts," growled the scalawag. And he came too.

The Boy's Story

One night an imp, a goblin, and a scalawag were feeling brave.

"I am so brave," said the imp, "I am going to do the bravest thing of all."

"What?" asked the goblin.

"Catch a boy!"

"Oh, boy!" cried the scalawag. "How?"

"In a hole dark as coal," said the imp.

"No. In a trap—snap," said the scalawag.

"No, no, no! In a bag," said the goblin. "I'd like to see a boy in a bag."

"Yes, that would be nice," the others agreed.

They put a big brown bag in the woods and filled it with pretzels.

"When something goes inside," they told their magic rope, "tie yourself tight around the bag. And don't let go."

Then they waited for a boy to come and eat the pretzels.

They waited and waited. No one came. It got late. They got hungry. So they started eating the pretzels, one by one—right into the bag.

Then—pop!—the bag closed, the rope tied itself tight, and—oh, mercy!—they were caught!

The three little things shrieked and hollered and bumped into each other because they could not see. Then the imp got worried that a boy would come and pinch them.

"We'd better go!" he shouted.

So they went. They went in three different directions. And so they went nowhere at all. But their little feet were so pointed and going nowhere so fast, they poked right through the bag.

Mercy! What a sight!

Then, sure enough, along came a boy. All alone. And by himself.

He saw something big and brown with six legs, looking fierce, sounding furious, and coming fast.

And did he wait to see what it was? Mercy, no!

Then the bag tore on a branch, and they all tumbled out—just in time to see the boy dash away.

"Scaring a boy is even better than catching him!" they sang and danced in the leaves.

"Was he really scared?" they asked when the story ended.
"Oh, yes," said the boy. "He was shaking like jelly."
Then the three little things howled. And they thought
that was wonderful.

"Now that we're friends," said the boy, "will you teach me to wiggle my ears?"

"Well, mercy, yes!"

So they wiggled and giggled all at once and showed him exactly how. And when he wiggled his own ears in front of the mirror, oh, my, how they cheered!

"Hooray and goodbye! Hooray and goodbye!"

Then they put on their little pointed hats, held hands tightly, quickly said, "Zinky, zinky, zoo," and—poof! They were gone.

And where did they go?

Well, I don't know.